The POKY LITTLE PUPPY'S
First Christmas

by ADELAIDE HOLL

illustrated by FLORENCE SARAH WINSHIP

 GOLDEN PRESS

Western Publishing Company, Inc.
Racine, Wisconsin

© 1973 by Western Publishing Company, Inc.
All rights reserved. Produced in U.S.A.

Library of Congress Catalog Card Number: 72-96318

GOLDEN, A GOLDEN BOOK®, and GOLDEN PRESS®
are trademarks of Western Publishing Company, Inc.

One winter morning, five little puppies tumbled out of bed and ran to the window excitedly. The whole world was white and sparkly. The trees were wearing silver lace, and there were little white caps on the fence posts.

"Snow!" cried the puppies happily. "Let's go play in the snow!"

"Very well," said their mother, "but remember— don't sneak away under the fence! And don't go running off up the hill!"

"We won't," they agreed.

But when their mother was busy with her work, one puppy spoke up. "Our mother said we couldn't go *under* the fence . . .

. . . but she didn't say we couldn't go *over* the fence."

Another puppy spoke up. "She said we couldn't go *up* the hill . . .

. . . but she didn't say we couldn't go *down* the hill."

"Let's go!" they shouted.

"Wait for me!" called the poky little puppy as he struggled through the snowdrifts.

The four lively little puppies ran and ran, until they came to a house at the bottom of the hill. They tiptoed to a window and peeked in.

"Oh, look!" whispered the first little puppy. "A tree! Not growing in the woods, but growing right inside the house!"

"And see the beautiful fruit on its branches!" whispered the second little puppy. "Not apples or peaches or pears, but *sparkly* fruit—all shapes and sizes!"

"And a star!" whispered the third little puppy. "Not shining in the sky, but shining at the very tip-top of the tree!"

"How pretty!" whispered the fourth little puppy.

Just then they heard someone coming. They turned and raced back up the hill, as fast as the wind.

Halfway up, they met the poky little puppy coming down. "Hurry home," they called to him, "and we'll tell you about the wonderful things we saw!"

Their friend Crow was perched on the fence, waiting for them. "Caw, caw!" he said. "I can tell you about the wonderful things you saw. I fly everywhere. I know everything that's going on in the world."

The five little puppies listened with shining eyes while Crow told them a marvelous story. He told them about Christmas trees and Christmas gifts. He told them about a jolly fat man in a red suit who comes on Christmas Eve.

That night, as they snuggled under the covers, the puppies made exciting plans. "Let's have Christmas," they said. "We'll write a letter to Santa Claus. And we'll go to the woods and find a Christmas tree."

But the next morning, their mother said crossly, "I saw muddy paw prints on top of the fence. And I saw puppy paw marks in the snow, going all the way down the hill."

The five little puppies hung their heads.

"Now, remember!" warned their mother. "Don't go *under* the fence or *over* the fence. Don't go *up* the hill or *down* the hill."

"We won't," they agreed.

But when their mother was busy with her work, one puppy spoke up. "Our mother didn't say we couldn't go *through* the fence—and I know a little place just right to squeeze through!"

Another puppy spoke up. "Our mother didn't say we couldn't go *across* the hill—and that's the way to the woods."

"Let's go!" they shouted.

"Wait for me!" called the poky little puppy as he struggled to squeeze through the fence.

The four lively little puppies soon reached the woods. They scurried about looking for treasures. They found a lovely, bushy green branch from a pine tree. They found hickory nuts, acorns, and bright red berries. They found thistle, milkweed fluff, hedge apples, and seedpods. And, they found cones—all shapes and sizes.

They were collecting their treasures, ready to start home, when the poky little puppy came bouncing up. "I may be poky, but I'm a good finder," he said. He held up a piece of shiny silver paper. "I'm going to make a star for the top of the tree," he told them.

That evening, the puppies hid their treasures under a bush. Then they wrote a letter to Santa Claus and put it up on the fence.

DEAR SANTA —
PLEASE BRING US WARM
SWEATERS, RUBBER BALLS,
AND LOTS MORE TOYS.
— THE FIVE LITTLE
PUPPIES

When they were all snug and cozy in their beds, the poky little puppy said happily, "Tomorrow is Christmas Eve, and that's when Santa Claus comes."

But the next morning, they found a sign on the fence, right beside their letter to Santa:

"Oh, dear!" they all said at once. "Maybe Santa Claus won't come at all."

They sat down to talk about being good. Each little puppy had something to say.

"Being good means
minding our mother—"

"And eating all our dinner—"

"And keeping our paws
and noses clean—"

"And going to bed on time—"

"And not running off
and leaving me behind!"
added the poky little puppy.

Crow flew down to join them. "Being good also means making others happy," he told them. "Christmas isn't just *getting*. It's *giving, too*."

The poky little puppy had an idea. "Let's give a party for our friends," he said. Then he had another idea. "But if we have to be good and stay home all day, who will invite them?"

"I will," said Crow. "I go everywhere and see everybody." And off he flew, with a loud "Caw!"

All that day, the puppies stayed close to home and were very, very good. That evening, they snuggled down happily when their mother tucked them into bed.

But when she was fast asleep, they got up quietly. They brought out the bushy pine branch and trimmed it with all the lovely treasures from the woods. Then they tiptoed back to bed—all but poky little puppy. He had one more thing to do.

He wrote on the letter to Santa:

AND LOTS MORE THIS.
—THE FIVE LITTLE PUPPIES

P. S. PLEASE BRING SOMETHING FOR OUR MOTHER AND FOR OUR FRIENDS, TOO.

Early the next morning, for the very first time in his life, the poky little puppy was up ahead of everyone else. "Merry Christmas!" he called excitedly.

All the other puppies tumbled out of bed and ran to the tree. "Santa *did* come, after all!" they called to their mother. "Come see our presents!"

"Caw, caw!" Crow greeted them as he flapped down and perched on a branch of a nearby tree. Brown Sparrow flew down, with a happy chirp, to perch beside him. Up scurried Gray Squirrel. Up hopped Rabbit.

It was a wonderful party, and there were presents for everyone. There were juicy bones and rubber balls and warm sweaters for the puppies. There were hickory nuts and acorns for Squirrel. There were weed seeds and juicy berries for Sparrow. For Rabbit, there were lacy carrot tops and crispy lettuce leaves. For Crow, there were sprigs of wheat and kernels of golden corn. And for the puppies' mother, there was a beautiful sweater and a lovely necklace of shiny red berries.

After she had admired her presents, their mother said, "Now *I* have something special for my five little puppies—something to help me keep track of them, so that I'll always know where they are going."

And around each puppy's neck she fastened a bright red ribbon and a tiny jingle bell!